GUIDE TO BEING GOOD

THIS BOOK BELONGS TO...

Look out for these Old Tom books . . .

GUIDE TO BEING GOOD

OLD TOM'S

GUIDE TO BEING GOOD

LEIGH HOBBS

Hyperion Paperbacks for Children
New York

First U.S. Paperback edition, 2006

10 9 8 7 6 5 4 3 2 1

Printed in the United States of America

Library of Congress Cataloging-in-Publication Data on file.

ISBN 0-7868-5694-7

Visit www.hyperionbooksforchildren.com

For Erica Irving and Dmetri Kakmi

"I'm tired of the same old faces at my garden parties," said the Queen with a sigh.

"Why not pick a name from the telephone book, Your Majesty?" suggested Sir Tassel Windburn, her able secretary.

"Splendid," said the Queen.
Soon the royal finger stopped at a last name
beginning with "T."

And so, when Old Tom went to collect the
mail one day,

there was a fancy-looking letter for
Angela Throgmorton.

She was enjoying a well-earned rest, having cleaned the house from top to bottom.

But this was a letter that couldn't wait.
A royal invitation for two, for afternoon tea.

Angela knew the Queen was fussy about
good manners. So she dressed up and wrote
back right away.

Angela had done her best to bring
Old Tom up nicely.

He often happily helped around the house,

and sometimes did two chores at once.

But now that he was to meet the Queen,

Old Tom needed extra instruction
on how to be good.

Angela invited a friend for tea.
"Pretend it's the Queen and
practice your manners," she said.

Old Tom had learned from his lessons that a nice smile is always handy.

He was eager to please and keen to be good.

So, when Angela's guest felt a little unwell,
Old Tom kept an eye on her.

Meanwhile, Angela went on with her eating instructions. "If offered cake," she said, "say 'yes, please' and 'thank you,' and don't drop your crumbs."

There was a lot to remember, but
Old Tom was pleased with his progress.

Though Angela felt there was still
work to be done.

In fact, Angela was desperate.

But time had run out, and Old Tom
was as good as he was going to get.

So Angela and Old Tom packed
their bags, and off they went.

Angela was excited...

. . . and so was Old Tom.

After his journey, Old Tom was tired.

PASSPORTS

"I've never seen anything like this before,"
said the passport man.

At the hotel,

Angela explained that she was on a royal visit.

Then, in the evening, Old Tom and Angela practiced their curtsies and bows.

Angela put on some gloves and pretended to be the Queen.

"Kiss my hand," she said.

In the morning, Angela got up bright
and early. Old Tom had to have a bath . . .

... and she was needed to remove the difficult oily patches.

This was a big day, and Old Tom planned
to look especially beautiful.

So, all morning, he combed and brushed
and fussed and even had his nails done.

When the arrival of lunch stopped him
in the middle of cleaning his teeth,

he still remembered his manners,
and gave a big smile.

Luckily, Old Tom's good looks hadn't gone to his head.

Angela, too, had spent hours getting ready.
Now it was time for afternoon tea.

So Old Tom and Angela caught a bus
to the palace.

When they arrived, Angela whispered,
"Now remember your lessons and you'll
blend in quite nicely."

Angela had expected there would be only
three for tea. But she was polite and hid
her disappointment.

Old Tom was on his best behavior,

while Angela began to introduce herself
and make polite conversation.

"Angela Throgmorton's my name," she said,
"and I'm here to meet the Queen."

"Aren't we all?" replied Sir Cecil Snootypants.

At first, Old Tom was a little shy.

But soon he relaxed and made himself comfortable.

Angela kept an eye on things and whispered
helpful hints when no one was looking.

Old Tom remembered to look people straight in the eye and make them feel special.

Then he had a rest from being good and
made himself a sandwich.

Being good had certainly improved his appetite.

Old Tom made friends quickly and even found a best friend.

He was careful, of course, to leave room
for dessert.

Meanwhile, Angela was having a lovely time.

"What an unusual hat!" mumbled Boswell
Croswell.

"I'm glad you like it," was her gracious reply.

The afternoon tea party was now in full swing.

"I hear the Queen has been delayed,"
said Lady Arabella Volcano to her
husband, Horace.

While chatting to Sir Basil Bossy and his
charming wife, Babette, Angela noticed
that Old Tom was gone.

She excused herself and began to search.
Angela tried to tempt Old Tom out with
a fresh chicken leg.

Angela described Old Tom to everyone she met.

"Oh, my goodness!" cried Sir Bertie Boodle.

"Good gracious!" shrieked Lady Winifred
Pineapple De Groote and her husband,
Sir Earnest.

"It can't be human!" cried Clarissa Cul-de-Sac just before she fainted.

Angela had lost
Old Tom, and wanted
him back before the
royal host arrived.

"By the way, where *is* the Queen?" asked
Sir Dalvin Dooper.

Suddenly there was silence, apart from
a tiny shriek from Lady Pineapple.

Her Majesty had arrived at last...

. . . and she had company.

Angela was thrilled to see Old Tom
and nearly forgot her manners.

But not for long, of course.

"So you are my *other* special guest! I've already met Old Tom," said the Queen. "And what jolly fun we've had!"

Her Majesty insisted that they stay the night.

After dinner there was a royal tour.
"That's my throne," said the Queen.
And then it was time for bed.

The comfort of her guests was most
important. So that...

... at breakfast, even if the Queen *had* seen
Old Tom's little mistake, she was too polite
to comment.

Goodbye!

Soon it was time to say good-bye. The Queen
had her royal duties, and Angela had to do
work around the house.

As for Old Tom, he was happy with a kiss
from Angela, his guide to being good.

1. A nice smile is always handy.

2. Always keep elbows off the table.

3. Look people straight in the eye
and make them feel special.

ABOUT THE AUTHOR

Leigh HOBBS

was born in Melbourne in 1953, but grew up in a country town called Bairnsdale. Leigh wrote and illustrated *Horrible Harriet*, which was shortlisted for the 2002 Children's Book Council of Australia Book of the Year Awards, in addition to the Old Tom books (*Old Tom, Old Tom Goes to Mars, Old Tom Goes to the Beach*, and *Old Tom's Guide to Being Good*). Leigh has two dogs, a blue heeler and a kelpie. He feels no affinity with cats, with one notable exception. Leigh lives in Australia but regularly visits the United States.

Visit www.leighhobbs.com

Join **OLD TOM**
on his next adventure!